one Two Follow Through

Starring Polly Pivot

by Mary Jacobs illustrated by Ron Noble

watercolor by Tracey Aston

It all started here in her Paw Paw's golf room,

for sweet Polly Pivot and her little red broom.

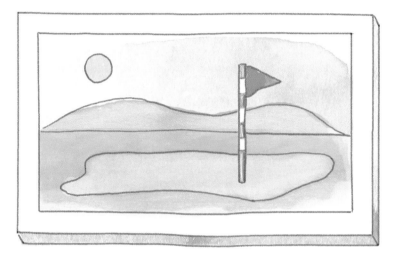

She aimed for the bin through all of his clutter.

A broom for a youngster was just the right putter.

Her face lit up and wore a joyful grin,

as ball after ball rolled straight into the bin.

Sweet Polly went on from sweeping to swinging.

She gripped her first club and she started FLINGING!

She held on so tight, but it leapt from her hands.

She cracked a wide smile as she *pegged* the tin cans.

Passion had a way of creating the right space,

to do what she loved no matter the place.

Her mother shouted, "Polly! Do NOT swing in here.

No more balls in the house, this had better be clear!"

Sweet Polly grew older and built a putting course,
with her Paw Paw's garage as the magical source.
She made hurdles and bumps and a few curves too.
Creating a challenge was all that she knew.

Her Paw Paw watched on as she played every day.

So proud and so clever - he had this to say,

"Stroke back on tick and through on tock,

and watch the ball roll right through the clock."

She made a device to keep her head from swaying,

and started to understand what Paw Paw was saying.

"Keep your head down and rocket your hip!

Relax those arms and just let 'er rip!"

It wobbled a bit - but she kept very still.

Paw Paw Pivot had never felt such a THRILL!

He said, "Oh me, oh my! You have wonderful flow!

Keep it simple, kid, that's all you need to know."

Two years later, Polly was ready for camp.

Every kid there had the look of a champ.

They all stood agape while a big fellow spoke,

with his GIGANTIC book, he seemed like a joke!

"I'm Greenskeeper Greenie - and I'm here to teach.

The golf pro is out to play Bubble Beach.

Just listen to me - I have seen EVERY shot.

The ONLY way to play is to swing like a *robot*."

They all piled in for a long, wild ride,

out to the range with their eyes open wide.

Greenie got speedy and gave camp some flair,

as the cart went up and caught sky-scraping air!

Polly sat in the front and soaked up the breeze,

while Greenie held his focus and landed with ease.

If chipping and putting did not make a mark,

the golf cart ride truly lit up that spark.

The campers got going and gave it a shot.

Some were naturals while others were – not.

But that's quite all right, just par for the course.
Polly Pivot was *RIPPING IT* with zero remorse!
Greenie looked on with a meanie Greenie face,
and noticed Polly's swing was a bit out of place.

He said, "Ms. Pivot! THAT swing will NEVER play.

Let's see what the robot guide has to say."

"First turn those pinky toes out to the side,

and bring in your feet – they're a wee bit too wide.

Then bend at your knees about eighteen degrees,

and give your bum bum a really good squeeze.

Now tuck your elbows deep into your ribs."

She thought, "Could Greenie be telling me fibs!?"

Her body froze and she lost all her grace.

She slammed the ground and mud splashed her face.

She sulked all the way home with tears in her eyes.

A game she once loved, she began to despise.

While thoughts to give up whirled around in her head,

some questions arose as she tossed in her bed.

"How does anyone get their swing back,

once a Meanie Greenie throws you off track?

Elbow tuck!? BUM BUM squeeze!? It's so confusing!

Which of these pointers should I be choosing?

Maybe there's a phrase to kick off my swing,

to quiet my mind and focus on one thing?"

After thinking and thinking and thinking some more,

alone late at night, she sat on Paw Paw's floor.

She read and she read – but nothing made sense.

The words were for grown ups and made her feel tense.

She thought, "Is this what Paw Paw reads all day?

There must be a simpler way to play!"

She set down the books and grabbed scissors instead,

and cut out pictures to see where they led.

A pattern arose from the photos she chose,

as each image showed the finishing pose.

Where there's a finish – there's always a start.

Following through set each one apart.

And look! It was done in all kinds of ways.

Which led Sweet Polly to this simple phrase.

One, Two, Follow Through,

and it applies to all that we do!

She went back to camp the very next day,
with pep in her step, she was ready to play!
Her Paw Paw was there in standard good cheer,
beaming with joy for his wee one so dear.

She carried her clubs, and her courage too,

with a gripping smile, she knew what was true.

But could she overcome what made her spirits sink?

And show what happens when we don't overthink?

She set up to swing and knew just what to do.

She counted **one**... then counted **two**...

And followed her way - all the way through!

She shared with her friends as camp came to an end.

And this was the birth of a *rippling* trend.

Sweet Polly Pivot sparked a whole new craze,

as they finished their swings in all sorts of ways.

Even GREENIE joined in and tossed out his book.

A magical phrase was all that it took.

One, two, follow through...

In all that we do.

One, Two, Follow Through
Practice Drill

WHAT YOU NEED: Very relaxed arms and a ball.

ONE: Pretend you are setting up to make a swing. Then turn your shoulders back over your right hip to the top of your backswing.

TWO: Fling the ball straight down in line with your back foot with dead arms (use your body) and give it some heat!

FOLLOW THROUGH: ALLOW the momentum to carry you all the way through into a balanced finish on your front leg.

ONE   TWO   FOLLOW THROUGH

*Right handed golfers hold the ball in your right hand.
Left handed golfers hold the ball in your left hand.

A Note from the Author

I grew up in southern Illinois, the youngest of six with five older brothers. Behind our huge yard there were acres and acres of cornfields, which I turned into a makeshift golf training camp. I blasted golf balls, picked them up, and did it again – and again. I made a tree course in our yard where I pegged branches, limbs and tree trunks. I even took the tractor and "lowered that lever" to cut little circles as my "green." I used a digging hoe as my pole and my mother's dishrag as my flag. Eventually, my oldest brother John took me to a real golf course and my life changed forever.

The concept of follow through applies not just to golf, but to everything we do. I wrote this book because I want to share this incredible game and its wonderful life lessons with children. I hope to inspire them to use follow through in their daily lives in order to become their very best selves.

To my mother and father for their endless love and
support, and for instilling the notion that helping
others brings true happiness.

My sincerest thanks to Kristin Walla for her
editorial inspiration.

This book is available in quantity at special discounts for your group or organization.
For further information, contact:
Triumph Books LLC
814 North Franklin Street
Chicago, Illinois 60610
(312) 337-0747
www.triumphbooks.com

Printed in U.S.A.
ISBN: 978-1-62937-895-4
Design by Classic Litho & Design